BERNICE
and the
Shadow Witch

WRITTEN BY

Brandt Ricca

ILLUSTRATED BY

Matt Miller

Ricca, Brandt. *Bernice and the Wonder of Pearl.*

Copyright © 2023 by Brandt Ricca

Illustrations by Matt Miller

Cover layout and book design by Liona Design Co., www.lionadesignco.com

Published by KWE Publishing: www.kwepub.com

ISBN (hardback): 979-8-9881235-0-7
ISBN (paperback): 979-8-9881235-1-4

Library of Congress Control Number: 2023918213

Acknowledgments

Brandt and Matt would like to thank those who have been instrumental in the *Barris Books* and *Bernice Books* series. Without them, and their belief in dreams and imagination, none of this would be possible.

Their AMAZING manager Kim Eley, Crystal Cregge, Adriane Miller, Brian Winterfeldt and the Winterfeldt IP team, Jonathan Thorpe, The Four Seasons Hotel-Georgetown and Linda Roth PR.

...and last but not least, all of their friends and family.

Table of Contents

Dedication from the Collaborators

"To my partner Chase, who's always next to me while I get lost in many dream worlds."

— BRANDT RICCA, AUTHOR

"To my dog Bailey...again. Because she deserves a second dedication."

— MATT MILLER, ILLUSTRATOR

1

———

Chapitre Un...

Without fear or vanity. Leaning into every moment thrown her way, seamless and unaware of it. That summed up the way Mrs. Hart waltzed through her life. It was a romantic dream, all of it, and she intended to enjoy it.

That's what Bernice thought, at least, as she peered up from her latest Agatha Christie book, *Death on the Nile*. It was the book after her last read, *Murder on the Orient Express*. Her gaze went from her joyous mother to the living room window. It was exceptionally cold that year in New Orleans and the Southern city was experiencing some falling snow.

• •

Though it wasn't sticking, to Bernice's dismay.

'Twas the night before New Years Eve and Mrs. Hart was still playing Christmas music and hanging new decorations for the big soiree she and her husband threw for the residents of Frenchmen Street every new year.

It may as well have been Halloween for Bernice: she fed off the history of the city she lived in. New Orleans was a city that was built on legends, stories of witchcraft, ghosts and vampires. It was full of eerie things. Her favorite author Agatha Christie kept her company with her murder mysteries and trying to figure out whodunit.

Nine year old Bernice had spent the summer before in New York City with her Aunties, Taflinda and Sarafina, and had explored every inch of the city with Jamay, her assigned chaperone and the Aunties' neighbor.

I was in my early years of being a Keeper. Me? I'm Gracie, a guide of sorts to all who enter... this story. Keepers monitor the dreams of sleeping children until they are ten years old, before they lose their childish enthusiasm. We guide them through their different dream worlds. Bernice was just one of my assigned cases, but one of my favorites.

I, for one, enjoyed guiding Bernice through her dream worlds all summer long, exploring NYC with her from afar. (Keepers can observe their assigned children when they are awake, but the children can not see or hear us.) I watched sparks of curiosity awaken in Bernice. As a young girl, Bernice was a Keeper's ideal assignment — no broken dreams for me to get lost in, yet at least, and always a solution to her problems that I could help with. Children can have broken dreams where a Keeper, like myself, can get lost, and never be able to return home to dream headquarters, Norizon, where all Keepers live and keep track of their assigned children.

The school year before, Bernice had been told that she would skip a grade, which would put her into her older brother Barris' fifth-grade class. (Barris was an old case of mine. He was over ten years old and no longer needed me.) He was not a fan of his sister being in his same class. But, when school began that fall, the teachers saw that Bernice was even smarter than they thought and suggested she be placed in the sixth grade. She was quite proud of herself, as were her parents, Mr. and Mrs. Hart.

Bernice happened to be reminiscing about her own intellect as she licked her finger and turned the page of her book, all confident.

"BOO!" Barris jumped up behind her.

Bernice threw her book in the air and at the same time Mrs. Hart let out a scream from the dining room.

"Mon Chere! You gave me a fright!" Mrs. Hart said as she finished hanging gold streamers around the dining room doorway. She loved any occasion where she got to decorate. "Now stop terrorizing your sister."

The Hart children were so embarrassed by their mother's holiday decorations. On the front porch, garland and poinsettias everywhere, Christmas decor flooding the yard, "Don't want Santa Claus to miss this house, dearios!"

• •

Mrs. Hart would say while she forced her four worker bees to help her: Barris, Bernice and their two older sisters Betsy and Betty, the twins.

"Do you really think the porch needs anything more, Mother?" Bernice said and looked at Barris because she knew he agreed.

"Oh nonsense, there are never enough decorations. Holidays come once a year, so once a year I shall make it count."

It was Friday and all the people of New Orleans were excited because that meant New Years Eve was on a Saturday, the weekend!

The older twin sisters were in their prime teenage years and were only concerned with looking attractive at the holidays for the boys they were going steady with, best friends Adam and Steve. Who didn't appear to reciprocate the magnitude of the twins' desire.

Bernice found it quite entertaining to watch the four of them when they were together. "How silly they are," she thought. All concerned with "foolish" things that were right in front of them and not the rest of the world out there.

Barris and Bernice watched the twins run out the door, laughing. "Bye Mother!"

"Be safe dears! And be home by curfew or your father will have a fit!" Mrs. Hart said as she added a new decorative table setting to her holiday display.

She placed the last red votive amongst its "friends,"

as she called the other candles, and rubbed her hands on her red apron. She looked very on-theme for the weekend. The red apron around her white, fluffy knee-length dress. Her pearls in loops around her neck, and completing the ensemble, her red curly hair tied up in a tight bun.

"Now... all is well," she said and returned to her apple-cinnamon-scented kitchen where she was baking up a storm.

Mr. Hart was working late and then planned to stop at Schwegmann's Grocery on the way home to grab pie supplies for his wife. More baking was on her schedule for the weekend and neither Mr. Hart nor the Hart children were going to complain about that. "Delicioso!" Mr. Hart would shout after what seemed like every bite of his wife's cooking.

She walked past Bernice and Barris in the living room. Bernice sat on the floor, as always, leaning against the sofa and reading. Barris played with the toy cars he liked to collect.

"And what will you be doing this weekend, dear sister?" Barris asked.

"I shall do whatever I want, brother. But it shall be a mystery indeed. To you, at least."

Their newest thing was to speak all prim and proper to each other. Mrs. Hart loved it and would try to join in, "I shall be preparing some delightful delicacies for the guests, my daughter and son."

Barris and Bernice would look at each other and wouldn't respond. Mrs. Hart was tickled with the "game" and would go about her business, amused at herself and

• •

clueless that she was the joke.

I observed the Hart family and marveled at how lucky they were. They didn't know it. Most people are oblivious to their good moments of life, especially the simplest ones.

There was a knock at the front door.

It was Pevy, Dean and Glenda, Barris' friends. They were waiting for Barris to ride their bikes around New Orleans in the falling snow and to see the fun holiday decorations before the residents took them down after the new year. They also wanted to see the fun costumes the locals, mostly the musicians who were playing on the street corners, were wearing. Glenda, Barris' friend and neighbor who was large in stature and always found with a treat, liked to leave candy in their hats, rather than money. "Musicians gotta eat," she'd say with a mouthful of what she was leaving them, mainly little candies.

"They're here Mother!" Barris didn't even wait for Mrs. Hart to respond and ran out the door to join his friends on his bike, while he threw on his jacket.

The door shut loudly behind him. Oliver, their fat Jack Russell Terrier, barked at the disturbance.

"Oh Olivier, shush," Mrs. Hart shouted. She had picked up her French language class again, and hadn't called their dog by his American name since. She always went back to her newfound French ancestry, which encouraged their move to the affluent French New Orleans.

"Did Barris leave?" Mrs. Hart asked Bernice.

"Mhmm," she replied with a tone that said he should've properly bid his mother adieu.

"Well, Bernice, who will you be meeting to go enjoy some holiday festivities?"

"Agatha, and she's right here," Bernice raised up her book.

"Oh that's nice dear. Glad there's room for another then."

Bernice stopped her reading at once and looked at her mother, "To whom are you referring?"

"There's a woman who just started working at the grocery and she and her family just moved here, the Cabini's. They're Italian. I can't remember where she said they moved here from, but they have a daughter who is your age. Her name is Ellie. They just live around the corner and I offered you up as her holiday gal pal this weekend."

"Mother!"

"Oh hush now, Chere, you need to get out more. And more importantly, you need friends. Those books you read don't talk to you. And socialization is good for you."

"These books *do* talk to me, and they tell me everything I need to know!"

"Hosh, posh." Mrs. Hart said.

"They're here." Bernice said.

Mrs. Hart stopped what she was doing and was confused.

A knock at the door came a moment later and interrupted their conversation. Bernice let the book fall to her chest with dread and looked at her mother.

• •

"What am I supposed to do with her?!" Bernice asked.

"Go and see Nona with the other children."

"The witch?!"

2

Chapitre Deux...

Nona Devereaux lived at 457 Frenchmen Street. While her appearance resembled what the neighborhood children thought a witch probably looked like, Nona was not a witch. She had a big nose, black shoulder length hair, and a forehead that Bernice described as "mean." It was wrinkly and moved up and down with her pointed eyebrows. Her voice sounded as if she had a frog stuck in her throat.

Nona lived alone since her husband had died a few years earlier, but, oddly, no one could ever remember from what. The many stories she had to tell gave her a reason to talk to people, whether they wanted her to or not.

She spun tales of Old New Orleans. There was the Vampire on Esplanade, the Voodoo Queen of the French Quarter, the Ghost of Bourbon Street, and the one she talked about that scared children the most: the Royal Street Witch. Royal Street was just a block away from where the Hart children lived.

"At night some say you can see a woman with red eyes and a pale face," Nona would explain, "floating and moaning around the streets, her black, ragged clothes hanging off her body. A woman scorned by her lover."

She would gesture wildly with her hands to emphasize her words as she spoke, garnering a collective gasp from the listening audience.

All the neighborhood children knew the tale of the Royal Street Witch and many of them were scared to go outside at night.

Nona lived in a dark red house, with three large windows

in the front that were accompanied by lime green shutters on each side. She had a wide front yard with items you would find at a flea market.

There was a wind chime made out of old Coca-Cola bottles hanging off a metal pole, a few old striped lawn chairs, a rusty fountain that had water and some fish in it. Too many little gardens to count. Her yard was very busy.

Each night Nona would go out to water her yard and to feed her fish, and when she did, the children in the neighborhood (at least those who weren't too afraid) would walk by and ask her to tell a story. More children would pause to listen as they passed by.

Mrs. Hart thought it would be a neat treat for Bernice to show her new friend some of the neighborhood and hear its stories from Nona.

"Bonjour Adriane!" Mrs. Hart exclaimed when she opened her front door.

"Hi Francine! Thanks for inviting us over, we are so excited to meet new people. This is Ellie," she motioned to the little girl standing at her side.

The little girl had black hair that was slicked and tied back tightly. She wore pants and a blouse tucked in, with an oversized brown coat. On her feet were black Mary Janes and black socks.

"Bernice, don't be rude, come and meet our new friends," Mrs. Hart called for Bernice, who was pretending not to notice the action going on. She continued to read.

• •

"Bernice."

Reluctantly, Bernice stood and walked to her mother. Bernice was not about the business of new people. Though she loved NYC and the things and places she discovered over the summer, back at home she found herself longing for anywhere but New Orleans and anyone... but the people there.

"Bernice, this is Ellie, who I was telling you about. I know you two will be fast friends."

"Hi," Bernice said, not enthusiastically.

"Hi," Ellie said, matching her tone.

"Now, Mrs. Cabini and I are going to chat over some tea. Why don't you take Ellie around the neighborhood and be sure to come back before dark."

Mrs. Hart patted Bernice on her behind and motioned for Adriane to follow her to the kitchen.

Bernice bundled up in her thick black winter jacket. The snow was still falling outside, slow and light. Nothing was sticking to the ground, but Bernice felt like she was in a snow globe. She loved the snow! But she hid her excitement for the weather from everyone.

"Do you want to go hear about some witches from Nona?" Bernice asked Ellie. She knew at that time, 4:30 p.m., Nona would be in her yard.

"Sure," Ellie shrugged.

Bernice walked out the door, ready to get the little meet-and-greet over. She led Ellie down the front porch and to the right. The two girls put their hands in their pockets to keep warm as they walked.

Bernice attempted small talk. "Where did you move here from?"

"We moved from outside New York City. Hoboken, New Jersey."

"I was in New York City all summer!" Bernice instantly became excited. "I explored all over the city, saw some Broadway shows, took the subway, and…"

Ellie cut her off. "Well aren't you just Miss Fancy Pants."

Bernice tried to laugh off the abrupt comment, "Haha, hardly, just did some New York City things."

"So, this Nona, what is she gonna tell us about?"

"She's just a bizarre old lady, likes to tell stories, and sometimes they're scary."

"Do you like scary stories?"

"I wouldn't say scary, but I love mysteries, which can be scary. I'm reading Agatha Christie right now, she's a favorite of mine," Bernice said.

"Oh, so you're fancy and smart." Ellie rolled her eyes.

Bernice was caught off guard by Ellie's rude behavior. But she didn't plan to be good friends with Ellie, so she didn't read too much into it.

Bernice and Ellie walked one more block before they got to the rotting old white fence that enclosed Nona's yard. Snow still fell slowly, like salt was being sprinkled on their coats.

• •

Nona was there talking to herself, throwing some food into her fountain for the fish. She had names for them. There were four.

"Eeny, Meeny, Miny and Moe, mummy's here with your dinner."

(Mrs. Hart was so tickled that those were the names of Nona's four fish. "That Nona is so clever," she would say.)

"Hi Nona, how goes it?" said Bernice, more confidently than she felt.

"Why hey Bernice, I'm good, knees are a bit achy today, which makes sense with the snow and cold."

Ellie laughed rudely.

Nona shot her a look, "And who is this little girl?" Nona's voice creaked like a door opening slowly.

"This is Ellie, she just moved here from up North."

"Well, a BIG New Orleans welcome to ya, bebe," Nona said energetically.

Ellie completely ignored her welcome, "So I hear you tell scary stories?"

"Oh I wouldn't say they're scary."

Nona opened a Coca-Cola bottle by wedging the side of the cap on the edge of her front step and hitting the top with her fist. When she finished this bottle, she'd add it to her bottle wind chime. There were almost fifty bottles hanging from three large metal poles tied together.

"They're more so tales of local history, that sometimes

• •

can be creepy. But that's with any city... but THIS city also has magic."

Oh how I loved when I got to observe Bernice with Nona, I loved hearing her stories too. I leaned next to the rotting fence and immersed myself in being an invisible listener.

"So what do you have to tell me today?" Ellie asked pessimistically, almost like a dare to Nona.

I was beginning to think this little girl was beyond rude. And I did not want Bernice to be friends with her. I made a grunting noise. Bernice looked in my direction, which was odd because children can't see or hear Keepers while they are awake. Only when they sleep.

Bernice looked back to Nona.

"Tell her about the Royal Street Witch," Bernice said. She thought it would be an easy tale to tell and to impress Ellie, who acted like she couldn't be bothered.

"The Royal Street Witch, eh?" Nona uttered with a whisper, but with a tone that showed she was excited to storytell. "Have a seat," she motioned to the teal and white striped rusty lawn chairs next to her fountain. She wiped the chairs with a towel from her porch: they were a little wet from the snow that was falling and still wasn't sticking.

Bernice and Ellie sat, ready for the performance.

"The year was 1925," Nona began, "and New Orleans was abuzz with the change of season. Fall was in the air, and celebrations would be happening for the next few months. People's moods are always better when it's time to celebrate.

"A local woman, Theresa, sat at a table in Jackson Square almost every day and would read fortunes of people who would pass by. She would dab a dot of paint on their cheek with a paint brush, and look at the dot, then read a tarot card. She would tell them truths of money that was coming, love that would be found, and revelations of who they were." Nona walked to sit in the third lawn chair next to Bernice and Ellie. She turned it a bit to face them.

"One night, a thick fog entered the square, causing most of the artists and residents to leave. You couldn't really see, except what was right in front of you. Theresa stayed, she needed to make money by reading fortunes. A man approached her table and sat down. 'Tell me who is the love of my life,' the man said to her. She looked at him, she felt her heart skip a few beats and butterflies overwhelm her. She dabbed a dot of paint on his cheek and flipped a card. 'I see someone with black hair, green eyes and olive skin.' Theresa had just described herself. The man looked at her and smiled. 'My name is Dimitri,' he said.

'I know who you are, I've seen you around these parts every few months. You ride in on the boats, come and go as the seasons.' She could hardly believe it but she was starting to feel what she had always described to others. Love.

Theresa and Dimitri spent the next few weeks getting to know each other, losing themselves in the other. They walked every inch of the French Quarter and everywhere they went, they heard music. The soundtrack of their love."

• •

"This is supposed to be about a witch, not love," Ellie interrupted.

"Shush," Bernice piped up. "Let her get to it."

"Then one night, Dimitri told Theresa to meet him at their favorite restaurant. He hadn't been able to see her for a week because of his work. She had been at the square all day, eager with excitement to see him. She closed up her table and hid it away in the bush like she normally did, storing it for the next day's work. She walked along the sidewalk, twirled to the violinist playing on the corner and played with her long black hair in her fingers. Then she walked around the corner of a building and saw Dimitri. She went to shout his name, but noticed he was with someone else. But not just anyone else, another woman. Black hair, green eyes, olive skin. She was dressed nicely and Dimitri was holding her hand outside of a jewelry store on Royal Street."

"Another woman?!" Ellie shouted.

"Indeed. Theresa confronted him, but he responded angrily, telling her he had found his true love, and her name was Lola. Theresa tried to cling to his arm and he yanked it away. She fell into a puddle from the force, fog was around her and she couldn't see. On the ground she heard Lola laugh and then the footsteps of the two of them walking away.

Theresa was in despair. Her hair turned gray and she grew pale from heartbreak and depression. Some say Dimitri had sucked the life out of her as he left by taking her love. Eventually she disappeared and was never heard from again. Another fortune teller found Theresa's table in Jackson Square, folded up in the bushes where she had left it. But folded into it was one tarot card, the card of Ghost. It is said that since then, all these many, many moons later, a woman with gray hair and a pale face can be seen, moaning through the streets, seeking her lover, and warning people she encounters who appear happy that their happiness won't last."

"All of that over a man?! I would never!" Ellie said. "When does this ghost appear?! What does she do to the children?!"

"The children who encounter her roam the rest of their lives like ghosts. You know she's about to appear when you see fog on the ground, like the night she was discarded by Dimitri. A tomb was established in Saint Louis Cemetery No. 1 for her when she vanished, a place for her friends to go and remember her. Tourists who seek revenge on others go to her tomb to express their harmful wishes."

"Where is it? I need to see this!" Ellie was becoming very interested. "What was her full name?!"

Nona stood up from her chair, took the last swig of Coca-Cola from the bottle and placed it on her steps. She would add it to her chime of bottles the next day. She walked up her front porch stairs and looked back at the girls. "Theresa Monroe." She opened the door and walked through, letting it hit the frame behind her.

• •

3

Chapitre Trois...

Flashback to Ellie before she moved to New Orleans

Ellie Cabini was a problem child. She liked to push buttons where she found them, she liked to break rules where they stood and... she liked to have company while doing it.

Her family had moved to New Orleans to start fresh. Ellie had become a girl of trouble three years before, and with each passing year she outdid herself. Her mother, Adriane, was warm yet worried for her daughter. She practiced yoga to relax and would play a record of piano music while lying in her living room doing so.

Her peace would be interrupted by Ellie, who bumped the record player on purpose when she walked past it. It was time for a fresh start, a new city, a new community. Mrs. Cabini thought the artsy atmosphere of New Orleans would allow her daughter to express herself and find out who she was.

Ellie also had a younger brother, Elliot. Elliot was Ellie's polar opposite, with a mature and positive attitude. He liked to correct Ellie's language: One would think he was the older sibling. He had blond hair, blue eyes and exuded sunshine. That's what his mother would always say, at least.

What had happened three years before was that Ellie had made a great friend at school, Lily, who then had to move away with her family. Once Lily had moved, Ellie never heard from her again. She had written letters, but nothing ever came back.

Her mother hated seeing her only daughter sad, so she took it upon herself to start leaving letters in their mailbox from Lily. She would tell Ellie that she mailed her letters to Lily, but she would read them and then write a response and place it in their mailbox a couple of days later.

Mrs. Cabini was elated to see Ellie happy when she read "Lily's" letters. She was able to practice her yoga in peace, and a positive environment inhabited their house again.

Until…

• •

One day Ellie was out playing with Elliot and had fallen, scraping her knee. She went inside the house to get a bandage and have her mother help her. But she interrupted her mother hidden away in a small room off the kitchen. She saw her there with the letters she had written, all of them, and saw her writing as she signed one, "Lily."

A dark shadow had been over Ellie ever since that only grew darker by the day. Her erratic and unkind behavior called for a change by her family. So to New Orleans they went.

Flash Forward to Ellie in New Orleans with Bernice

"Live a little, Bernice," Ellie said as she and Bernice stood outside Nona's house. "We have to go find Theresa's tomb."

"I'm not supposed to be out past dark, my mother will be expecting me. And it's really cold out," Bernice said, as she wanted nothing more than to be home and curled up with her book.

Bernice was hoping she would run into her brother Barris and his friends, a distraction that would be helpful.

"What's the worst that would happen if you're a little late?"

Bernice thought how Mrs. Hart never really punished her children, rather just spoke to them in a "life lesson" tone and then offered an anecdote. Her mother did want her to make friends, after all, and here was an opportunity staring her in the face.

Ellie could sense Bernice's will slowly giving in.

"Nona said Cemetery No. 1, right?" Ellie asked.

Bernice nodded.

Saint Louis Cemetery No. 1 was the most famous and oldest cemetery in New Orleans. It had tons of spooky residents, all with spooky stories. Stories of those who loved and lost. Those who dreamed big... and those who were notorious for voodoo and criminal behavior. It was not a great place to visit in the dark. But Ellie Cabini had listened, and became enthralled, to Nona Devereaux.

As I watched Bernice and her new friend hail a cab to the cemetery, I started to get a bad feeling.

Bernice relished a cab ride, and loved how Ellie had the money to pay for it. Ellie seemed so adult. It reminded Bernice of being back in New York City when she wasn't with her parents.

"You girls be safe now," the cab driver said as the back door closed behind Bernice and Ellie.

Standing in front of the cemetery's black gate, with its white stone wall surrounding the above-ground crypts, Bernice felt goosebumps crawl over her skin.

The street light above them illuminated the entrance, but once inside, it was just the dim gray sky and the faint moon above the clouds that lit the way for the two girls. Snow continued to fall.

"Theresa Monroe, she said. Now how do we find it?" Ellie asked Bernice.

• •

"I haven't any idea. There are so many here, and I don't think they are in any particular order."

Due to the frequent flooding of the city, stones and shells had been placed on top of graves to prevent them from washing away during storms.

While I watched Bernice and Ellie, I saw a dark shadow emerge from behind a crypt and float, like a wave of darkness, over the two girls. It was gone just as fast as it came.

"I don't think we should be in here," Bernice said. She started to walk backward out of the cemetery and didn't take her eyes off Ellie. "You need to come back with me, now."

As Bernice tip-toed backwards, I waited to see if Ellie would go with her. She needed to be a good friend. But something was at Ellie's side. Shadow dust. I immediately felt fear take over and my stomach in my throat.

Shadow dust hails from Shadow Witches. It is purple, and shiny and is the mark that a Shadow Witch has been with a child. Keepers can't ever see the actual witches themselves when a child is awake, but the dust is what clues us in that a child's witch is active. It's like a footprint.

Every child has Shadow Witches that live within them. They represent bad behaviors. Once one becomes awakened, they awaken the other witches that reside in the child. There is one for every bad quality a person can have, such as, the Witch of Resentment, the Witch of Bitterness, the Witch of Cruelty. There are many that are in a person, although they don't always wake up if a child's *good* traits overpower them.

· ·

Once a Shadow Witch awakens the others, those witches surround the child and persuade them to show more and more poor behavior. They feed off any negative circumstance that occurs in a child's life, whether it's loss, discomfort, a major change. Shadow Witches are what Keepers have learned causes a child's broken dreams.

My grandmother Lucy, a great Keeper of the Universe, became lost in a broken dream years ago, and I still haven't been able to figure out how to rescue her.

The more a Shadow Witch and the others tempt the child to misbehave, the more broken dreams they have, and the darker their shadow becomes. A Keeper can become lost in the maze of the broken stormy dreams, disconnected from the child, and can be trapped in the child's shadow, alone. And seeing that pile of purple shiny dust that lay under falling snow in the cemetery, I knew we were not alone.

I heard a wicked storm of whispers. A terrified Bernice, who appeared to hear them too, ran out of the cemetery, leaving Ellie.

4

Chapitre Quatre...

Bernice lay in bed that night, amazed at how a simple evening could go wrong. All she had wanted to do was stay in from the cold and read Agatha, but her mother had other plans... and so did her new friend Ellie.

In her warm bed, dressed in her cozy pajamas, Bernice looked out the window and saw snow, still falling.

She had run away from Ellie, jumped on the first trolley home that she saw and ran inside her house as fast as she could.

"My goodness!" Mrs. Hart exclaimed when she saw Bernice shut the door behind her.

"Where's Ellie?" Mrs. Cabini asked.

"She said to tell you she would just meet you at home." Bernice heard herself lie and immediately felt anxiety and shame.

"I guess that's for the best," Mrs. Cabini said. "It's getting late and Ellie hates to be out in the dark."

Bernice shut her eyes tight. "If she only knew her daughter," she thought. She could feel tears beginning to come as she pictured Ellie standing alone in the cemetery. She was a horrid little girl, but Bernice had left her in the dark.

"Oh Adriane, it was so great to get to chat!" Mrs. Hart showed Mrs. Cabini to the door. "We must see you and your family tomorrow for our New Year's Eve party. You'll get to meet all the other neighbors."

Bernice watched the fog form on her window from bed as she tossed to lay on her side. She wondered about what mischief Ellie had brought to the Cabini's house. She was too upset to read Agatha Christie that night; the book lay unopened next to her pillow. She didn't even tell Barris or her sisters about what had happened, not knowing yet what to make of it.

At last her eyelids grew heavier and heavier with each passing minute. She fell asleep hearing her parents laughing downstairs as they enjoyed their "lover time" — what they called the time for themselves when the children were all in bed and they played their records and danced.

Remember, each child enters their dream universe based on their surroundings when they fall asleep. Bernice's brother rode the musical notes of Frenchmen Street into his dream universe. A little girl named Jade rode into hers on gusts of wind in the city of Chicago, and a little boy named Michael would ride the echoes of wolves, as their howls vibrated through the air on his ranch in Yellowstone, Montana.

Bernice was a big reader; she was always surrounded by books. When Bernice fell asleep each night, her walls would start swarming with words from her favorite books. They would circle like a tornado rising up the walls, then pour onto her like water, scooping her up and carrying her out of her window.

Tonight, Bernice was carried away just as she always had been.

Bernice wakes up in her dream world

When she opened her eyes she saw a dark sky with faint stars shining. She appeared to be inside a room, but it had no roof, only grand walls.

Bernice was surrounded by four walls that made up a very large marble room. There was a marble floor with a large swirl on it, pillars and dim chandeliers. You couldn't make out much but the faint architecture of the space.

I popped into the room to meet her.

"Hey there!" I exclaimed, excited to see my favorite child. I held onto my black beret and big brown jacket. All Keepers wear trench coats (to keep our supplies, in case we need them while helping a child), mine was large and was my grandmother Lucy's, and we have knee-high striped socks. All of us Keepers' eyes are purple because of our devotion

• •

BRUCE J.
AVERY C.
CODY C.
BRITTANY W.
DANIEL M.
JULIE S.
BENJAMIN G.
KIMBERLY C.
JEN M.
MATTHEW M.
BRENDAN K.
REEMA A.
BERNICE H.
JUSTIN M.
CLAUDIA S.
JAMES C.
JULIE W.
JOSEPH I.
EDITH G.
ZOE C.
NADIA M.
HARRIET R.
DEMI M.
VICTORIA B.
SHAYNNA F.
LILLY S.
BRITTANY H.
YOSOUF H.
JULIA O.
MYLA M.

to dignity and wisdom, and magic. My eyes sat beneath my red spaghetti hair, which illuminated my Black skin.

"Hey Gracie!" Bernice said, still looking around the room.

My excitement to see Bernice was quickly overshadowed by an uneasy feeling.

All of a sudden we heard a loud storm of whispers, that almost hurt our ears. They grew really loud and just as quickly as they came, they stopped.

Then, we heard what sounded like a loud finger snap.

The chandeliers burned brighter above us and showed us we weren't alone. We stood in a large ballroom with others who appeared to be frozen in the middle of a dance. A fog began to cover the floor.

Bernice grabbed my hand. She was scared. (I didn't feel all that comfortable myself.)

A gust of wind blew through and then a dark shadow floated over us. Music began playing.

The people resumed what one could assume was a waltz.

There were men dancing with men, women with women, women with men, and some others that were more ambiguous.

Masks covered all their faces and all were dressed in elaborate, weird clothing, with feathered shoulder pads, scarves, and many layers of fabric. Almost homely, but a fancy form of homeliness in colors of brown, black, dark green and burgundy. Their legs glowed as if they were made of lights.

• •

Above everyone hovered a throne in mid-air, with a woman sitting in it. She looked peculiar and had a long curved nose. She sat there floating above the crowd with her eyes closed. Short feathers grew where her eyelashes should have been. She was seemingly unaware of — and not caring — what was happening below her.

"Where are we?" Bernice asked me.

"I'm not sure, all I know is that I was with you tonight when you were with that wretched girl, Ellie. Then I went back up to dream headquarters in Norizon, and I saw that your bulb was flickering."

In the middle of Norizon sits a big board, almost like a switchboard. It is as large as it could be and is filled with light bulbs. Each bulb represents a child's dream world. Different colors mean different things. When a child has a broken dream and a Keeper becomes lost, the color turns to black before it flickers out. The bulb then fills with black smoke. Normal bulbs of normal children are all different colors, but you want to avoid black.

Bernice's bulb that night was purple, then started flickering from purple to gray, which was worrisome.

The people around us didn't acknowledge our presence, but continued with their waltz to what sounded like a symphony playing. We could see no musicians.

I noticed the dancers all had glowing legs. Fog on the floor prevented us from seeing their feet.

"Something is very weird here," Bernice said.

"Isn't 'weird' the curiosity of life?" said a crackling voice that came from a woman twirling with two others. The woman stopped dancing as she twirled to be in front of Bernice and me.

I stood in front of Bernice to protect her. I felt very uneasy in that world.

"Oh don't fret, eager defender. I won't do anything to you here. It's out there you have to be worried about," said the woman.

She was dressed in a glittery brown smock and had a small curved nose. Her hair was plaited in many black braids that were then coiled in a bun on top of her head. She had big hair, but it wasn't as big as the woman who floated above us.

"What do you mean, out there?" I asked.

"Why, *out there*, when the child is awake of course."

"Edwina, that's enough," said a loud, but slow whispering voice. It echoed in the ballroom.

We then heard a swarm of whispers that appeared to be coming from the floating woman. Her eyes remained closed and her lips didn't move.

"Pardon me, Enchantress," Edwina cowered. Her peers continued to dance unphased.

"Take them to the Knowing Hall. And stay there," said the Enchantress from above, eyes still closed, lips unmoving.

"This way, pretty girls," Edwina motioned for us to follow her.

• •

"Who are you?" Bernice and I asked at the same time as we followed Edwina through a rippling brown door, leaving the others dancing.

"Why, I am Edwina, the Witch of Mischief," she said proudly. "I am a Shadow Witch."

• •

5

Chapitre Cinq...

"A Shadow Witch?" Bernice asked.

"They are all that is bad." I said to Bernice in a whispered voice. I didn't want Edwina to hear me since we were still following her from behind.

"It's OK, she's right." Edwina turned around. "We hear it all as well," she said with a smirk. Sparkles floated around her curved nose.

"What do you mean all that is bad?" Bernice inquired further.

"Why little girl, we are persuasion in the form of poor

behavior. We need it to thrive. And from the looks of the Knowing Hall, your persuasion is starting to stick." She raised her right arm slowly to point at the long circular red hall we were entering.

Down the hall were dim lights, with gold glowing picture frames hanging on both sides of each wall.

In the frames were images of Bernice and things she had done — the result of bad decisions she had made. In some frames it looked as if the picture was still forming, and other frames were empty.

Bernice came to one picture frame, and the image she saw inside was still very fresh in her mind. It was of her and her new friend Ellie, getting out of a yellow taxi, in front of an eerie cemetery.

"That just happened!" she said and looked at Edwina.

"It did indeed, and I was there."

"I knew it! I saw the purple dust," I shouted to both of them.

"Purple dust?" Bernice asked.

"It's the mark of a Shadow Witch who has been with a child while they are awake. But just like children can't see us Keepers when they are awake, we can't see Shadow Witches around children."

"That's right," Edwina nodded at me, becoming excited and skipping playfully around us. "Each child has a Shadow Enchantress. The woman floating in the ballroom. She becomes aware when a child is around poor behavior, or when they may be influenced by poor behavior. And then, one by one, she cues all of us dancing in the ballroom to leave the party and to go out into the child's world and persuade them to make mistakes, sometimes awful ones. We can even touch objects and influence the world, not only the child."

Edwina pranced around like an excited child while telling her story. "Once the dance floor is utterly empty, then the Enchantress awakens herself, and leaves her post to fully immerse herself into the child's life. And that is when awful things occur, everything bad you can think of that a person can do. There's cruelty, committing crimes, living selfishly, being mean to friends and family. It's unfortunately a business that keeps us busy. When our work is done and the Enchantress is awake, she absorbs all of us and we strengthen her power."

Bernice looked as if she were about to cry. "So... am I becoming a bad person?"

"You have a ballroom full of Shadow Witches, still dancing, which means you have done a diligent job of not letting things affect you," Edwina said. "Until tonight."

I took Bernice's arm and turned to face her. "I knew that Ellie was bad news! She was up to no good making you go to that cemetery, I just knew it!"

"It was but a moment, Bernice," Edwina said reassuringly. "A moment of you hearing a story that you've heard a thousand times about a witch, but this time a new listener suggested something that you knew you shouldn't do.

· ·

And your ambition to make her like you triggered you to go. Honestly, you were an easy target, when I was summoned by the Enchantress to go to you."

"How did you, or how do you persuade children to do bad things?" Bernice asked.

"By doing this." Edwina had disappeared in front of our eyes and Bernice was now hearing her at her side, whispering in her ear. Her hand touched Bernice's shoulder and sparks started to appear.

Bernice jumped. Her ear tingled from Edwina's whisper. She rubbed her ear and shook her head.

"All you have to do is whisper?" I asked.

"That's right, and touch your shoulder to send vibrations," Edwina's voice sounded hollow and eerie. It gave me and Bernice goosebumps. She appeared again in front of us.

"A slither out there, and a whisper in here," she pointed to Bernice's ear.

"Why aren't you still outside in the world? Why are you back here dancing if you all disappear one by one out there?" I pushed her with questions.

"Bernice so far is good. She, as any child, has the tendency to be led by others, but she didn't follow through with her mischief, so I didn't get to finish my job. But whenever children do horrid things, the evidence appears here in the frames of Knowing Hall. That's how the Enchantress keeps track of bad behavior."

Flashback to Norizon, Dream Headquarters

Lucy, a great Keeper of the Universe, had been lost for a year now. Her granddaughter Gracie, along with her grandmother's friends, Neo and Simone, could typically be found in the Elklis of Norizon researching how to rescue her. The Elklis was where all records of dream headquarters were, and the history of all Keepers.

"We know broken dreams are caused by Shadow Witches, but what we don't know is how to piece a broken dream back together, which would allow a Keeper to get back to Norizon," said Neo.

Neo was Lucy's best friend since they were little and were Keepers in training together. His father, Nevarre, had also become lost in a broken dream many years before. Neo had been on the path of rescuing him and all lost Keepers ever since.

"I think the answer lies within THE Shadow Witch, the head enchantress," Simone said as she studied a page of an ornate old book on a table. "The Enchantress is the key, to get the other witches to somehow stop fully existing in a child's reality. Once the Enchantress is awakened and out in the world herself, it's too late."

Their purple eyes read the page, which described how broken dreams occur.

"So we need to find a child who hasn't had all of their Shadow Witches cued yet to reach the Enchantress?" Neo looked at Simone. "Specifically the children my father and Lucille were assigned to?"

"Exactly right. Now to figure out how we know if a child hasn't had all of their Shadow Witches cued, since we can't see them. Just their little pile of dust after they're gone. We need to track down those kids."

A younger Gracie sat among stacks of papers, pretending to fully understand what was happening. She was overwhelmed with grief, missing her grandmother, who had taught her everything she knew: how to love, how to live simply, how to just sparkle. "Happiness is always having something to look forward to," Lucy used to say to Gracie.

Up there in stacks and piles of books, papers and bankers lamps... all three of them looked forward to rescuing Lucy and Neo's father.

Fast Forward to Bernice, Gracie and Edwina

"We all have within us the same traits. Good, bad and evil," Edwina was saying. "The difference between children is who acts on those urges, feelings and thoughts."

"Pardonnez-moi!" A woman stood by the red circular wall. Her outfit matched the wall and she had blended in. We started to see her silhouette as she turned toward us and then we saw her sparkling black eyes. She must have been there the whole time.

"Who are you?" I asked.

The woman was giggling and acting playfully, like Edwina. "I'm Granya, the Witch of Chaos!" Her giggle echoed through the room.

6

Chapitre Six...

Granya moved with urgency, but at the same time as if she had no place to be. She wore a glittery red garment that appeared to be torn. It shimmered, whereas before, it had blended in with the wall. It fell to her knees, above legs that were glowing subtly, on and off. Her feet were unseen, as the floor was covered in fog, even in the Knowing Hall.

"I'm gonna be a star!" she shrieked in a high pitched voice that made her sound on the verge of insanity.

"It's almost my turn out *there*. And, well, I never miss my mark." She walked slowly in a circle around Bernice and me, leering at us with crazy eyes. "The Enchantress shall be pleased with my work."

"How are you about to go out *there*?" Bernice asked. "Aren't you Chaos?" And then turning to look at me, "Am I about to cause chaos?!"

In Norizon, dream headquarters, they start us Keepers young with our training, led by Grelda the dream universe witch. Nothing that I had learned in Grelda's classroom prepared me for this moment, or this night. Not many Keepers had interactions with Shadow Witches. I wished that Simone and Neo were with me to help navigate the Shadow Witches.

"You're not chaos, Bernice."

"Oooooh, naive child," Granya chimed in, "we all are chaos, it's about who acts on it. And I plan to make sure girlie here puts on a show!"

"Oh bite that tongue Granya, it may not be your turn yet," Edwina said. "And I still have to finish up my mischief assignment. The photo on the wall is only half developed." She pointed to the glowing picture frame and the image of Bernice and Ellie at the cemetery.

"You may be right Edwina, but my legs are flickering and we both know what that means. My time is almost here."

Bernice and I looked down at Granya's legs and she was right. They did flicker, but there were seconds between each flicker.

"What makes something your time? Your time to go out *there*?" I asked the two Shadow Witches.

"Come with us, and you shall see." Edwina led us down the red Knowing Hall, past frame after empty, glowing frame.

It was a long walk. Some areas were dark and we heard faint thunder. Leaves floated up from the fog-covered ground past us, but seemed to disappear into the darkness

above our heads. Slight whispers swarmed around us, and we saw little glowing white sparkles appear and disappear along the dark walls.

"They're watching," Granya giggled.

"Who are they?" I asked, needing to know quickly. It was creepy.

"The others," Edwina answered. "Some witches lurk here in the shadows of the walls and are on standby to assist their fellow Shadow Witch should they need it at the meeting."

"The meeting?" Bernice asked in a small voice. She was scared and hung onto my arm. I was scared too, but it was the whispers that gave me goosebumps.

"The meeting at the corner of *good* and *persuasion*. It is with every child and it is how we enter their reality and supply our dark wishes."

As we walked along the darkness, leaves and whispering voices, we approached a shimmering light. It was a revolving circle of gold sparkles, like a hollow globe, and we stepped into it.

"Here we are, this is your *good*," Edwina said looking at Bernice. "This is where we intersect areas of your life, with our persuasion."

Edwina began to spin, her curved nose and the sparks around it starting to shine brightly. The sparks multiplied, soon covered her body, and she disappeared.

"That's how we get to you," Granya whispered in

Bernice's ear, startling her.

A gust of wind blew through the air, and Edwina appeared again with a flash of light. The sparks that revolved around us froze for a moment, then continued their twirl.

"We come to where your *good* is, all your good qualities and traits, and we stand here in the middle as we are now, and flicker into your world to push influence. If we need help, the witches on standby in the shadows accompany us. Power in numbers, my dear."

"Why would you need their help?" I asked.

"If a child's *good* is too strong for our influence and persuasion, then additional witches can help us overpower their *good*. The witches in the shadows have powers of all sorts, while those who dance with the Enchantress are assigned just one trait, as I'm Mischief and she's Chaos." She raised her nose, pointing to Granya.

"But I was unable to finish my task with you, child, even with the help of the whispering witches. What makes you so special?" Edwina walked toward Bernice to examine her.

"Don't touch her," I said, stepping in front of Bernice.

"Oh hush, Keeper. This one's unique and I want to know why, and so does the Enchantress."

Flashback to Bernice*

Bernice Hart had always been an ambitious little girl. She kept her nose in her books and also in her own business.

• •

Her mother Francine knew her daughter was special — not in a way that every parent thinks their child is special, but in a way where she sensed something powerful in her daughter. The way Bernice always knew when something was wrong and knew when company was coming. When Bernice would be searching for a lost item or book, she would turn around and it lay before her. One time Mrs. Hart caught Bernice sleepwalking while she waved her hand around creating a glowing aura. Mrs. Hart convinced herself it was a reflection of some light somewhere, though no lights were on.

"The street lights from outside," she reasoned to herself.

But what Mrs. Hart didn't know was that her daughter had a Keeper named Gracie, as did her son. Mrs. Hart didn't remember that she once had a Keeper herself... but that's a story from long ago.

When Bernice is awake, and Gracie, her Keeper, observes her, Bernice could sense her presence. She felt it in New York City at a theater, when she was visiting her Aunties the summer before. And she felt it that day in Nona Devereaux's cluttered yard.

When visiting her sick grandfather, Paw Paw Leo, where he was staying for his dementia, he pointed his finger at her when she walked into his room.

"Get that bright light out of here! That one right there!" He shouted and became upset when he saw her. The nurses calmed him and then he seemed to come back to himself and recognize his granddaughter.

• •

Whether it was her introverted demeanor, her comfort with characters in books rather than people, or her intuition that always seemed to be a coincidence... Bernice Hart was a little girl who was not like others she knew.

Fast Forward to Bernice, Granya, Edwina and Gracie

"I'm going to be unique too!" Granya shouted in her shrill voice. She disliked not having the attention on her.

"I don't know what you mean," Bernice answered Edwina's claim. "I am no one special."

"Maybe not, but you are... something. I shall find out when you are awake and have another go at you," Edwina said.

"Or it'll be me! Edwina's legs aren't even flickering anymore." Granya pointed to the Witch of Mischief.

She was right. Edwina's legs had not blinked once since we had encountered her. The witches in the shadows started to whisper louder as Granya continued pointing, and then she began her high pitched giggling.

The whispers got louder; we covered our ears.

7

Chapitre Sept...

"What's happening?!" Bernice shouted.

Edwina and Granya seemed unfazed by the deafening voices.

I kept supplies in the black beret on my head (you always need to be prepared). I reached above each ear and pulled down flaps from my hat to cover my ears. Bernice looked at me enviously.

Granya started to prance around the spinning sparkles. "Our friends are not happy you are here," she said creepily as she twirled and jumped.

. . . .

"We never have the child we are influencing in this area with us," Edwina said quietly.

The whispers seemed to settle and an echo of them retreated down the hall we had just walked.

"There is something about your presence that doesn't sit well here, child." As Edwina spoke the fog started to disappear, revealing a green floor that we had been walking on. We still couldn't see the witches' feet. Theirs were blurry.

"I am so confused by all of this," Bernice said, shaking her head and looking at me. I had no answers to give. But just then Bernice clutched my arm again and I remembered: I had a new ability. I could remember forgotten things when I touched an object or someone had touched me. And then there it was, a memory.

Flashback to Norizon, Dream Headquarters

Neo was tired from reading the countless books and papers in the Elklis. He was in a corner sitting in a big brown leather chair that seemed to swallow him. His trench coat acted like a blanket.

Simone came to him from the other side of the room. The candles burning at every table were melting down. Other Keepers in training entered the room to start replacing them.

Keepers in training perform all sorts of tasks around dream headquarters; it earns them certain privileges while in training.

"Why don't you call it a night? All this will be here tomorrow," Simone said to her friend. "You can research more with some rest."

"I just can't bring myself to give up," Neo said, stretching in the chair. "I even feel guilty for sleeping or taking rest. While I am here to operate at my leisure, my father and Lucy are somewhere, lost." The book he was reading fell to the floor.

A younger Gracie had fallen asleep on a stack of books nearby. After Keeper training each day with Grelda, the dream universe witch, her extra curricular duty was to hang out with Simone and Neo. She wanted to find her missing grandmother, just as Neo wanted to find his father.

"Eloise, right?" Gracie would ask when turning pages of the books of children with broken dreams. She would look up to Simone or Neo to confirm each time. "That's the name of the little girl who Grandma Lucy got lost in her broken dreams?"

Simone and Neo would nod yes each time.

Neo walked past Gracie and patted her head to wake her up. "Thank you for your help today Gracie, but you should get some rest too."

Neo walked out of the Elklis to head home. Gracie stood up and rubbed her eyes and looked at Simone. Simone was studying a page from the book that Neo had let fall to the floor.

• •

"What do you see?" Gracie asked. She could see that Simone had stiffened as she read.

"It looked as if," Simone paused to read some more and turned the page, "there once was a connection made in the early 1900s of a little girl who was able to help Keepers."

"What do you mean?"

"It appears that her assigned Keeper, Dottie, was able to connect with her while she was awake *and* asleep," Simone eagerly read, "Dottie was able to communicate with Evelyn, her assigned child, and she helped her with her other assigned children who were having problems."

"How was Dottie able to see Evelyn and talk to her while Evelyn was awake?"

"It doesn't say... this looks like it was being documented by Dottie herself and then it stops." Simone turned the page but found that the rest had been ripped out. And there was a small sparkling purple stain on it.

Gracie touched it, but it was dry. Simone shut the book abruptly.

"Isn't purple the sign of a Shadow Witch?" Gracie asked Simone in a whisper.

"It is, but there's no way a Shadow Witch could've been here. They reside within the child. Unless..." Simone stopped. Gracie tugged at Simone's coat, wanting answers.

"Unless Dottie had this book with her while she was in the dreams of her children, and a Shadow Witch got a hold of it to prevent us from knowing what Dottie discovered,

· ·

and Dottie brought it back here unaware of the missing pages. Let's go to the Storik!"

Simone grabbed Gracie's hand and they ran to a place Gracie hadn't seen since the night her grandmother went missing.

The Storik is where pictures of all the Keepers who have been lost are hung in memory and in hope of being found.

Fast Forward to Bernice, Granya, Edwina and Gracie

I mentally went back to Bernice; she was standing in front of me.

"Gracie? Gracie? Are you OK?" She shook my shoulders. Granya stood off to the side, giggling and frolicking among the sparkles. She created little gusts of wind among them, which stirred them in the air. The Witch of Chaos' purpose was always to stir up trouble.

I told Bernice of my memory. She was too distracted by what was happening to take it all in.

Edwina appeared to be talking to the whispering witches; she fit the description Witch of Mischief well.

She nodded her head and then her eyes widened. "We must go to the Enchantress," she said. She looked at Granya and made a face that meant business. A wind swept through the area and the floating sparkles started to shine brighter, a cue for those in the shadows to start their loud whispers again.

- -

"We must go now, the Enchantress will know what to do," Edwina said. She pushed Granya forward and motioned for Bernice and me to follow.

"What do you mean?" I asked urgently. The mood was shifting to something disturbing, something wicked.

Granya twirled and giggled as we walked away from the corner of *Good* and *Persuasion*. It was too eerie to stay down there with only the whispering witches as company, although they filled the entire hallway in the shadows.

Edwina whispered to the witches and Granya continued to giggle, looking back at us now and then to make sure we were still there.

"I'm feeling icky about this," Bernice said. She looked from right to left and stayed very close to me in the middle of the hall. We held hands tightly.

"I'm afraid if I stand too close to the walls, one of them will grab me," she whispered in my ear.

"I am scared of that too," I admitted.

Bernice and I followed the Shadow Witches. When we approached the glowing but empty picture frames on the wall, the frames started to shine brighter, and as we walked past them, they fizzed like sparklers on the Fourth of July.

Granya's voice shrieked, "Oooooh, so pretty!" Her giggles became hysterical laughter.

"It's not a good thing!" Edwina interrupted her fun. " The Enchantress will know what to do. They said that it is very vital and she isn't who she appears to be."

• •

"Who's she? And who's they?" Granya asked, giggly.

"The girl," she motioned to Bernice.

"And the witches on the walls... And their friends."

"There were more than just witches there?!" I asked, feeling more scared than I had ever been.

Edwina squinted her eyes and spoke in a low hiss. "Yes. Why, there are many things in the shadows. One always needs everything in the dark."

• •

8

Chapitre Huit...

As Bernice, Edwina, Granya and I were about to walk through the rippling door to exit the Knowing Hall, a bright blue light flashed in front of us. All four of us covered our eyes.

"Grelda!" I shouted. Grelda appeared before us, with her long glowing cape and blonde hair coiled in layers on her head. Her yellow skin was bright with the reflection of her cape. I was never so happy to see her as I was at that moment!

"Who are you?!" Granya's voice was even more shrill than before. She laughed and the sparks around her curved nose started to spin.

"That's THE Universe Witch," I explained to the Shadow Witches. They both looked at each other, and then to Grelda.

"Hi Gracie and Bernice. We don't have much time. I was in Norizon, at the board before going to teach my class of Keepers in training, when I saw Bernice's light start blinking fast."

• 8 •

"The board?" Bernice asked timidly. "My light?"

"The board in Norizon, the Dream Sani (SAN-NYE) is where we see all the dream worlds of sleeping children," I explained. "It's like a big board of lightbulbs, and each bulb is a world. When the bulb changes colors or blinks or goes out in smoke, we know something is wrong."

"And yours was blinking Bernice, dear, which I have only seen once before," Grelda said in a kind rush. The rippling door we stood in front of parted down the middle and opened as if it expected us to walk through.

"Bring her," a voice that filled the entire space whispered

loudly around us.

Grelda seemed startled and hovered down a bit at the sound of the voice, "It's the Enchantress," she grabbed Bernice and me and tucked us into the sides of her cape.

"Stay close to me, these witches can't be trusted, they're unpredictable with their magic and whispers."

Edwina and Granya skipped ahead of us as if they were going to a party, and while skipping ahead they would look back at us to make sure we weren't far behind.

"The Enchantress is eager to speak," Granya twirled and skipped, giggling, as sparks played around her.

We walked through the rippling door and were back in the large marble ballroom. The dance of the other witches was still going on. They all seemed to be dancing in slow motion this time, and while the fog was gone, their feet were blurred. Like Edwina and Granya's.

Music played in the ballroom, a song that Bernice and I knew, one that she played on the piano before: "Clair de Lune." The song seemed to be a theme in her life. The Shadow Witches danced slowly together, unbothered by our presence, beneath the roofless room, dark skies and clouds above. Not a star in sight now.

We walked through the crowd of dancers. Bernice looked closely into one of the witch's sparkling black eyes as they stared at another. Their curled nose had sparks like Granya and Edwina's, but they too moved in slow motion. Bernice touched a spark and it moved slightly with the tip of her finger.

• •

The Enchantress floated above us, eyes still closed.

"She won't open her eyes to us, so don't worry. All of the other witches have to be awakened before she is able to see us," Grelda said, trying to comfort both Bernice and me.

Granya and Edwina arrived at the front of the ballroom and stood in front of and below the Enchantress.

"Voila, Enchantress," Granya squealed. "Hope you are pleased!"

"You've done wickedly," she whispered in response. "Now bring the girl forward so I can have a look at her."

Grelda, who knew some of what an Enchantress of Shadow Witches could do, but knew she probably wasn't yet a direct threat, wrapped her arm around Bernice and held her close.

"What do you want with this child?" Grelda asked.

"She shouldn't be here," the Enchantress replied, "Something is quite peculiar about her indeed," her voice cracked in a whisper. Sound of thunder started above.

Grelda also knew that it was odd for a child to be in the Shadow Witches' realm. A child would typically be able to be near them only when the witches were persuading them in their reality.

"Whatever the case, we must be leaving here at once. We have no business with you, witch." Grelda spoke matter of factly, holding her ground and showing confidence.

"Bring her closer," the Enchantress hissed to Edwina and Granya who slithered toward Bernice.

Grelda and I stood protectively in front of Bernice.

"You stay back now, you hear!" I held my hands up, along with my fists.

Suddenly the marble floor beneath us started to slide away, forcing Grelda and me against the dark walls, and separating us from Bernice. Hands reached out from the dark walls around the ballroom to restrain us and the whispers began again.

Bernice was being held by Edwina and Granya and she struggled to get out of their grip.

"Closer," the Enchantress beckoned to her obedient Shadow Witches. "Closer," she whispered again.

As Bernice continued to resist, a necklace she wore started to glow. The glow grew brighter with each moment.

"Ohhh," Granya giggled, "So pretty."

"Get that necklace off of her!" the Enchantress shrieked. Wind gusted through the ballroom, and the sight of lightning began.

"Let me go!" Bernice shouted, squeezing her eyes tight and pulling against the witches' grasp.

A bolt of lightning flashed and everything went blindingly bright.

Shadow Witches shrieked from every corner.

• •

9

Chapitre Neuf...

Bernice opened her eyes. She was back in her bedroom at the Hart residence, in New Orleans on Frenchmen Street.

She felt a wave of anxiety evaporate when she realized she was in the comfort of her bed, surrounded by her books. "Oh Agatha," she thought, feeling a sense of safety with it. She felt as if Agatha Christie was her friend from reading her so often.

Outside it was a dark morning and the snow was still falling. It was now covering the ground.

"Oh my!" she said out loud, bringing her hand to her

heart with excitement. And then she felt her necklace, a simple gold chain on which hung a pendant in the shape of the sun. The memory of what happened with the Shadow Witches started to come back to her.

"Was this necklace special?"

"Why did it start glowing?"

"What happened to Grelda and Gracie? And those awful Shadow Witches?"

Bernice shuddered and felt goosebumps. The temperature had dropped outside and Mrs. Hart had not adjusted the heat yet in the house.

A bookshelf filled with books took up an entire wall in Bernice's room. Stacks of more books lay on the floor.

The books started to shake and some popped open, their pages turning.

"Gracie?" she asked as if she knew I was there.

"Hi Bernice," I said casually as I walked from behind the bookshelf from inside the wall and stood in front of her.

"What are you doing here? How can I see you?"

"All will be understood soon," I told her.

"What happened, am I still dreaming?"

"You are awake and indeed not dreaming."

Bernice was still clutching her necklace.

"It all leads to this," I pointed to the chain she held. "It begins with your family, Bernice. You see, after you exuded light and left the realm of the Shadow Witches inside of you, Grelda and I were transported back to Norizon."

Bernice sat up on her bed.

"It was back in dream headquarters that Grelda had told me of myths that Keepers have always been suspicious of, but never have confirmed, until last night with you."

"You see, knowledge can present itself as a story unfolds. With your act of light, some pages magically reappeared in Norizon, and graced us with things that could help us mend broken dreams. With that, Grelda became versed in your story and that of your family."

"What are you talking about?" she asked.

"You come from a line of prophets of sorts," I went on. "A line that can help Keepers with troubled cases, broken dreams and communication. You can see and talk to us when you are awake and sense Shadow Witches. It's your special gift, an intuition, so to speak."

"In my family? My mother has never told me about any of this." Bernice stood and started to pace anxiously.

"She doesn't know. It skipped her generation, BUT, her mother Evelyn was one. It all started with her."

"Evelyn? I'm named after her, it's my middle name. Bernice Evelyn Hart. And this was her necklace. I never met her, she died before I was born."

"That's right, she was a helper to her Keeper and their other assigned children. Although, it is very rare. We have never known of another one or if the stories were even true. The only case was a Keeper named Dottie who had experienced it."

"Dottie! THAT Evelyn is MY Evelyn from that book! The story you told me!" Bernice exclaimed.

"Yes! But Dottie was figuring it out and documenting it, when a Shadow Witch got her book, and those pages. She made sure that all of it disappeared, along with Dottie in a broken dream."

"Oh my gosh." Bernice abruptly sat down again, trying to digest all this new information.

Bernice had always felt different from other children. She loved stories and getting lost in them, and she could sense things that others couldn't. She had always chalked it up to, well, just how she was.

"Bernice, there is something you need to know." I gently touched Bernice's hand.

"You are now my only hope of rescuing my grandmother, Lucy. She was lost a couple of years ago in a little girl named Eloise's broken dreams."

"What am I supposed to do?"

"A child who has many broken dreams has a dark shadow following them and dreams of nothing. Because they dream of nothing after a while, they can't connect with Keepers, which means a Keeper can't get into their dreams to help those who are lost."

"OK...?" Bernice said. I could tell she still needed more information.

"Now that you and I can communicate when you're

awake, I need to find where that little girl Eloise lives and we'll go to her. And I will tell you what to say to her and help her *Good* overcome the Shadow Witches. But we need to do this before the head Shadow Witch, the Enchantress, wakes up within her. Then all will be lost."

Bernice nodded. "Alright, but I need to get a grasp on all of this. I went to bed a book worm and I woke up having powers and being a Keeper's solution to broken dreams."

"I understand," I told her. "Do you want to know what magic feels like?"

Bernice nodded slowly.

"Let me show you." I grabbed Bernice's hand and showed her a vision from my memory. The entrance to Norizon where all the seasons change as you walk. All the Keepers in the many levels there, practicing their abilities, Helfie the Norizon concierge handing out assignments at the dream board. The Keepers floating, disappearing and reappearing. Then the laughter of my Grandma Lucy, and her relaying a story of how she helped a young boy, Neo, who needed a friend when his father became lost.

"That's magic Bernice. The work we do, who we are and the way we help others." I was standing next to Bernice in her mind, as I watched her stare at my memory and the wonder that was Norizon.

Bernice's eyes opened. I was standing in front of her again in her bedroom.

Bernice exhaled, fingering her necklace that had newfound meaning. She was lost in thought.

• •

"My mother always says magic is that feeling you get right before you laugh. When everything starts bubbling up inside of you and you feel it here." She pointed to her chest.

A knock interrupted us.

"Bernice! Time to eat!" Mrs. Hart exclaimed. "I have whipped up a hot breakfast to keep you warm with all this snow!" Mrs. Hart walked back downstairs, humming merrily as she went.

Bernice looked at me and started to change out of her pajamas. "I've got to go."

Fin...

Downstairs at breakfast Bernice sat in silence as her siblings told their stories of being with their friends, and their parents went over the guest list for their New Year's Eve party that night. As usual, music filled the Hart residence. Ella Fitzgerald graced their breakfast table and provided some warmth on what was a cold morning.

Bernice looked toward the staircase as I came down the stairs. She now could see me while I observed her reality. She had become awakened within herself.

Bernice looked back to the pancakes, untouched on her plate.

"What's wrong Chere?" Mrs. Hart asked.

"Nothing. I couldn't sleep last night. It was cold."

"That's my fault, I'm not used to this winter wonderland weather and forgot to adjust the heat."

"Perhaps your books can keep you warm," Barris said

sarcastically, taking a bite of bacon.

"Oh no need, Cheres, I have totally forgotten that we have three fireplaces. No need to use them much in this 'Nawlins' weather. But your father will be getting some wood today to set the scene for tonight! Isn't that right dear?"

Mr. Hart had taken a gulp of his milk that left him with a white mustache. He took another big gulp. "That's right, anything to make my love happy," he said. Mrs. Hart bent down and gave him a kiss. She patted the milk from her lips from kissing him with her napkin.

I walked around the Hart dining table and bent down to smell the delicious food. Mrs. Hart poured love into all of her cooking. It gave me and everyone who ate it the feeling that nothing could go wrong.

***

The day had gone by with the Hart family doing what they were told by their mother. Cleaning here, decorating there and ensuring the house was the picture of party perfection.

Bernice hadn't spoken much that day; reliving her dream the night before and everything I had told her as she carried out the tasks ordered by her mother. She momentarily got lost in the love affair of her parents when Mr. Hart had finished stacking wood in the fireplace and lit it. Mrs. Hart clapped her hands to applaud his efforts and he grabbed her mid clap to dance with her in front of the fire.

Ella Fitzgerald's holiday record had been playing all day and she sang for Mr. and Mrs. Hart. All four of the Hart children were alternately pleased and embarrassed by how happy their parents were.

I especially enjoyed watching love at its finest.

Bernice found herself relaxing, watching her parents, until a shadow entered the closed living room window and rolled across her parents.

She felt goosebumps and looked at me.

I swallowed hard. We needed to find Eloise soon, I thought.

Mrs. Hart giggled. "Alright children, run upstairs and get ready. The guests will be here shortly!"

Everyone stood around, not feeling the same level as her excitement.

"Now shoo! Shoo!" She hurried them along waving her hands.

The Hart children went to their respective rooms. Bernice rolled her eyes hearing her older twin sisters Betsy and Betty talk about how they'd dress. "Oh what are we going to wear? Everyone will be looking at us!"

Bernice made a face behind them. Her sisters thought they were so gorgeous. Well, they were, but they didn't need to flaunt it like they did.

Bernice was standing at her large mirror. She had put on a navy dress with a white belt and smoothed her long black hair away from her face with a white headband.

She adjusted the skirt of her dress and then stared

at her reflection. I was hovering at the side. "Don't you have other children than me to bother?" she asked.

"I haven't received any new assigned cases today, and none of my current ones have any other problems. So, being as you're my only child who can see me when awake, and we have an important job to do together, I'm gonna stick around to see what happens."

Bernice let out a sigh, "Well, just don't be in my way, the last thing I need is my family thinking I'm crazy."

"Aren't you going to ask your mother about your grandmother, Evelyn?"

"No." Bernice walked to her door to open it. "I will, just not today. She's so happy, and if she learns about her mother, it will scare her. Let her have tonight. It's her night."

I nodded in agreement.

***

The party was a smashing success. The neighbors and friends of the Hart family all enjoyed the food, the music and dancing.

Barris hung out all night with Dean, Pevy and Glenda, his three best friends. Betsy and Betty took turns complimenting each other and seeking compliments among the guests too.

Bernice sat on a large red chair in the corner of the living room, next to the fireplace as the fire roared. She still felt cold though. The snow continued to fall outside, but it

had lessened and some stars had begun to appear through breaks in the clouds.

Suddenly, Bernice saw her. Ellie Cabini had walked in with her family. She stood at the front door, diagonally from Bernice in the corner and waved at her. The Cabini's removed their winter coats and shook off the snow.

Bernice viewed Ellie as reckless and didn't want to see her just then. She was too busy thinking about Shadow Witches and glowing necklaces.

I stood next to Bernice, eyeing the chocolates Mrs. Hart had put out, when Ellie walked up to Bernice. "This should be interesting," I thought.

"How goes it, Bernice?" Ellie said as if nothing had happened the day before.

"Hi Ellie. I take it, you made it home OK?" It was more of a statement than a question.

"I did, no thanks to you. You left me there and I had to jump on a trolley to make it back before my mother got home. But don't worry, I'll take you back there again to find the tomb of Theresa Monroe."

Bernice chuckled and looked at Ellie, "You think I am going to go anywhere with you again? You almost got us in trouble, and for a dumb story you heard from Nona."

"Oh life is more fun with a little trouble Bernice. Live a little. I'll teach you soon enough."

Just then, Nona Devereaux walked up to Bernice and Ellie.

"Did you enjoy my tales of witches yesterday, girls?" She felt like she was a local celebrity and relished whenever she had listeners.

"Oh we did, Nona, you're quite the storyteller," Ellie said, but in a sarcastic tone.

"Oh now, I have many more you'll like, Eloise." Nona took a sip of her eggnog and giggled. She appeared to have indulged in the eggnog a bit too much.

At that moment I heard nothing in that house. Everything went silent and it was as if the crowd of party goers didn't exist.

"Why'd you call her that?" Bernice asked, startled.

• •

"Why child, that's her name," Nona laughed, "Don't you know who your friends are?" Nona giggled and walked away to rejoin the adults at the party.

"I thought your name was Ellie?" Bernice questioned the girl.

"It is. Well, it's my nickname. My real name is Eloise."

I looked at Bernice who looked at me.

In that second, in front of that fireplace, on a dark snow-filled night, there it was.

Grandma Lucy was lost in a broken dream. A broken dream of a troubled little girl named Eloise. And she was there in front of me, in that tall green house on Frenchman Street.

Just then the countdown to the New Year started. "Three... two... one... Happy New Year!"

Confetti and applause. And a little bit of hope.

. . . .

Author

Brandt Ricca is a D.C.-based entrepreneur. Having a writing background and a family history of owning a newspaper, telling stories has always been at the forefront of Brandt's mindset.

Creating a narrative is a must for Brandt, who always wants to convey a message with events or imagery through his branding agency, Nora Lee by Brandt Ricca.

Brandt was born in Baton Rouge, Louisiana, and loves the Southern culture and creative atmosphere of New Orleans, which inspired the setting for the life of Barris Hart.

illustrator

Matt **Miller** is a designer and artist that bounces back and forth from D.C. and Florida. For as long as he can remember, Matt has had a passion for expressing his ideas and creativity in drawings and paintings. His artistic background and love for interior design and architecture are the foundation for his interior design and rendering business, Perspective.

With a soft spot for historic architecture of the American South, and gathering inspiration from his own vivid dreams, he felt he was the perfect fit for illustrating the world of the Barris Books series.

www.ingramcontent.com/pod-product-compliance
Lightning Source LLC
Chambersburg PA
CBHW040103150726

48005CB00013B/1561